Penny Dreadful
and the
World Record
page 97

Meet Penny Dreadful and her Resigned Relations...

Penny
(It's never really her fault...)

Cosmo
(Penny's best friend)

Georgia May Morton-Jones
(Penny's genius cousin)

Daisy
(Penny's annoying sister)

Penny's long-suffering mom and dad

Very prim-and-proper **Aunt Deedee**

Barry
(Meow, I'm Gran's cat)

Gran
(Normally found fast asleep somewhere)

...her Crazy Classmates, and Sick and Tired Teachers

Bridget Grimes
(Star student)

Mr. Schumann
(**SICK AND TIRED** principal)

Henry Potts
(Cosmo's mortal enemy)

Sundwich fan,
Alexander Pringle

Miss Patterson
(Penny's tall-and-thin-like-a-beanpole teacher)

Shaves-his-head-every-week
Brady O'Grady

Cherry Scarpelli
(Bridget's best-friend-forever)

Luke Bruce
(Puts things up his nose)

Penny Dreadful
Versus the Vampire

My name is not actually Penny Dreadful.

It is Penelope Jones. The "Dreadful" part is my dad's **JOKE**. I know it is a joke because every time he says it he laughs like a honking goose. But I do not see the funny side. Plus it is not even true that I am dreadful.

It is like Gran says, i.e. that I am a **MAGNET FOR DISASTER**. Mom says if Gran kept a better eye on me in the first place instead of on *No Nonsense Nanny* at 2 pm on LifeTV then I might not be quite so magnetic. But Gran says if Mom wasn't so busy answering phones for Dr. Cement, who is her boss, and who has bulgy eyes like hard-boiled eggs (which is why everyone calls him Dr. Bugeye), and Dad wasn't so busy solving crises at the city council, then they would be able to solve some crises at 73 Rollins Road, i.e. our house. So you see it is completely not my fault.

For example, it is not my fault that Mr. Bentley-Bucket is **SOAKED TO THE SKIN** and smelling like garlic. If it is anyone's fault it is, e.g.:

a) Miss Patterson's, who is our teacher, and who is tall and thin like a beanpole, for telling me to **STOP** trying to balance a pencil sharpener on my nose and to **START** thinking about how long it will take a mouse to run around a table, or I will grow up to be a complete **CLOWN**.

b) Cosmo Moon Webster's, who is my best friend, even though he is a week older than me and a boy, for saying he does not want to be a **CLOWN** when he grows up, he wants to be a **VAMPIRE HUNTER**.

3. Aunt Deedee's,
for not making it completely
clear that Mr. Bentley-
Bucket is not even **PART
VAMPIRE**.

★ ☆ ✹ ✦

What happens is that we are in math and we
are all supposed to be concentrating on how big
is a table if it takes a mouse ten seconds to run
around the edge. But Henry Potts, who is
Cosmo's mortal enemy, is saying a mouse should
not be on a table because of the **GERMS**
(because he is very into what has germs on it
and what doesn't). And Cosmo is saying Henry
Potts should not be even **NEAR** a table because
of **HIS** germs, which are worse then a mouse's.

And I am saying,

> Look I am balancing a pencil sharpener on my nose and it has been there for five whole seconds, it is **AMAZING**.

And Henry Potts says,

> Isn't!

And Cosmo says,

> Is!

And then Henry Potts throws an eraser at Cosmo, only it hits my pencil sharpener and knocks it off my nose, which I say is a **TRAGEDY**. But Miss Patterson says it is not, it is what you get if you mess around with pencil sharpeners on noses, and if I do not concentrate on the mouse I will end up as a **CLOWN** instead of, say, a teacher or a doctor or a nurse.

Only I say I do
not want to be
a **CLOWN**, *or*
a teacher or a
doctor or a nurse,
I want to be the
fastest roller skater
in the whole world,
because I am very into
roller-skating fast, even
though Dad says it is a **MIRACLE** I have not
broken my legs, and Mom says it is only a
matter of time…

And then almost immediately everyone is
going **CRAZY** with what they want to be when
they grow up, i.e.:

a) Alexander Pringle, who wears age 14 clothes even though he is nine, says he wants to become world champion for eating the most sandwiches in ten minutes.

2. Brady O'Grady says he wants to be Wayne Plane, number one soccer star.

iii) Cosmo Moon Webster says he wants to be Minimus Mayhem, leader of the Herobots.

4. Henry Potts says he wants to be an evil zookeeper who will invent a half-monkey/ half-crocodile beast to rule all beasts, and to kill Minimus Mayhem.

Only then Cosmo says he will invent an evil werewolf, which is half-man/half-dog, who will battle the half-monkey/half-crocodile to the **DEATH**.

BLOOD

So Henry says he will invent a were**MOSQUITO** that will suck the blood of the werewolf until the **DEATH**.

And Cosmo says he will hunt down a were**GIRAFFE** who will stomp on the weremosquito until the **DEATH**.

And in fact the only person who wants to be a teacher or a doctor or a nurse is Bridget Grimes, who is the star student in our class and Mr. Schumann's favorite, and who says the answer is seventy-eight inches as long as the mouse does not do any swerving.

Only by then no one knows what she is talking about, not even Miss Patterson, who says she wishes she had been a nurse when she grew up, and also that it is time for climbing ropes in PE so to **STOP** thinking about evil beasts and **START** thinking about putting our shorts on without any more **SHENANIGANS**.

Only Cosmo **CANNOT** stop thinking about evil beasts and the next day on the way home from school he says he is not going to be Minimus Mayhem, leader of the Herobots, after all, he is

going to be a vampire hunter because he has a book from the library and it tells you everything you need, which is:

a) A notebook, for writing down anything **STRANGE**.

2. A camera, for photographing anything **STRANGE**.

c) Garlic, to scare the vampires with.

4. A wooden stake, to stab through the hearts of the vampires with.

e) A hat, because it makes you look important.

And I decide I would like to be a vampire hunter when I grow up too, because I am into hats and garlic and looking important, which is when I have my

which is to hunt down a vampire and then we can take it into school for show-and-tell and it will be the best show-and-tell **EVER** (even better than the time Bridget Grimes brought in the piece of moon in a glass box), and then Miss Patterson will not think I am a **CLOWN** at all.

And Cosmo agrees, and so we go back to his house to get the notebook and the garlic and the camera and the hats (which are actually a cushion cover and a policeman's hat), and the wooden stake (which is actually a chopstick from Jade Palace takeout). And also some cookies, which are not in the book, but I am feeling hungry and so is Cosmo and we agree if our tummies

rumble then they will scare the vampires away.
And then we go to the graveyard, because
vampires are always in graveyards or shut-
down factories or haunted mansions, and we do
not have a shut-down factory or a haunted
mansion, so it is the graveyard or nothing.

And so we are sitting on a wall eating our
cookies and waiting for vampires to show up,

and so far we have photographed and noted a lot of **STRANGE** things, i.e.:

a) A dog with a fan-shaped collar, which Cosmo says is because it is a ghost dog from olden days, only Shaniqua Reynolds from the salon says it is because he has a sore ear and is not allowed to scratch it.

b) Barry, who is Gran's cat, and who is usually on the sofa watching horse racing, not in graveyards.

Cosmo says it is because he is actually secretly a werecat and could battle us to the **DEATH** any minute, but I say it is because Gran is in the bakery next door and he is waiting for an eclair even though Mom says it is **CAT FOOD AND CAT FOOD ONLY**.

3. Mrs. Butterworth, who works in the post office and who has a mustache and a beady eye and who says,

What are you doing lurking in a graveyard with a cushion on your head, Penelope Jones?

And Cosmo says, "We are hunting evil beasts and eating cookies." And Mrs. Butterworth says, "Well don't get crumbs on the gravestones or there will be rats and I will report you to Reverend Bruton," who is the pastor, and also the dad of Elsie Maud, who got Alexander Pringle's head stuck in the railings.

And me and Cosmo agree that Mrs. Butterworth is definitely **STRANGE** and possibly **BEAST**-like but she is not a **VAMPIRE**. I say this is **DISAPPOINTING** and maybe we should photograph somewhere else, e.g. the town hall, which has a creaky door and some bats on the porch. And Cosmo agrees, so we are about to go completely quickly to the town hall when someone comes out of the church and it is a man who is tall and in a blue suit and Cosmo does a **GASP** and says,

It is **DRACULA**, king of the vampires.

And I say it is not, it is Mr. Bentley-Bucket
(who is Aunt Deedee's new boyfriend, and
who Gran says will not last, it is the same as
nannies, i.e. that they all get fired for **NOT
MEASURING UP**, except Lilya Bobylev, who
has been fired twice but
Mom got her unfired
because it was mostly
my fault) and he is
NOT an **EVIL BEAST**
he is a **SAINT**
for putting
up with
Aunt Deedee,
according
to Mom.

Plus vampires do not wear blue suits, they wear long cloaks with a red shiny lining.

But Cosmo says that the blue suit is his mortal disguise, because Cosmo is very into mortal disguises, and that  underneath he definitely has on a long cloak with a red shiny lining and we have to follow him and find his **LAIR**, which is probably under a tombstone, which is where he goes to sleep. Only I say I can't because I have to go home because Daisy, who is my sister, and who is very irritating, is being doubly irritating because she has decided she wants to be a celebrity chef when she grows up and so she is cooking macaroni and cheese for dinner. And Cosmo says in that case can he come, because he is very big on macaroni and cheese, because his mom (who is called Sunflower, even though her real name is Barbara) does not believe in eating creatures, because it is **OPPRESSIVE**. She believes in cheese and nuts and squishy things made of lentils. So I say yes and off we go.

And on the way Cosmo is saying how **FORTUITOUS** it is for Georgia May Morton-Jones (who is my cousin, and who goes to the Drabble Academy for Girls), because if Aunt Deedee marries Mr. Bentley-Bucket, then she will have a new dad who is a vampire. And he wishes Sunflower would marry a vampire or maybe even Minimus Mayhem, only she doesn't believe in weddings because they are **OPPRESSIVE**. And I am thinking it would be really good if my dad was a vampire instead of something to do with safety bollards, because then he could fly and hang upside down in trees, and Bridget Grimes would be in **MORTAL FEAR** of me instead of saying *"I would not do that if I were you,"* when I notice a **STRANGE** thing. The **STRANGE** thing is that Mr. Bentley-Bucket is not climbing under a tombstone to go to sleep, or wandering off to Aunt Deedee's house to play chess with Georgia May Morton-Jones, he is completely **FOLLOWING** me and Cosmo down the road.

He follows us past the dead
pigeon behind the general store.
And he follows us across the cross walk with the
marshmallow stuck on the stop sign from when
Brady O'Grady and Cosmo had a
marshmallow-throwing competition (only
Cosmo's hit Mrs. Butterworth and she is never
selling him marshmallows again,
not even when he is nine).

And he is still following us when we walk up Rollins Road and down the sidewalk and to the door of Number 73, which is our house.

And I am banging on the door and Cosmo is shouting,

Quick, quick he is going to **DEVOUR** us any minute, Janet. Open the door and call the police.

And Mom does open the door but she does not say, "Oh my **HEAVENS**, a vampire!" and she does not call the police, she says,

How many times, Cosmo? **STOP** calling me Janet. It is **MRS. JONES**, and I suppose you are staying for dinner too? Well you had better scoot and wash your hands because Aunt Deedee is here. We are all meeting Mr. Bentley-Bucket. Oh heavens, here he is. **PLEASE COME IN**.

And he **DOES**.

And then Cosmo and me are completely
DISCOMBOBULATED and also **FLABBERGASTED**
because there is a vampire in the dining room about
to eat macaroni and cheese and also possibly **US**
but no one else is even one bit **SUSPICIOUS**. Cosmo
says it is because he has them **UNDER HIS SPELL**
and we need to **REVEAL HIS TRUE NATURE**
and also his red cloak under the mortal disguise.

Which is when I have my next

BRILLIANT IDEA™

which is to reveal his true nature at dinner by
giving him the garlic and some water, because
Cosmo says vampires do not like garlic and
water, it makes them **EVAPORATE INTO SMOKE**,
and so does being stabbed in the heart with
wooden stakes, only we have dropped the
chopstick down a drain trying to poke a worm,
so it is just the garlic and water.

Only when we get to the table there isn't any
water, there are **STRAWBERRY SMOOTHIES**,
which we are not normally allowed to have
because of the time I put "hormones" in them and
made Daisy's boyfriend Joshua Bottomley sick,

even though Daisy is not in love with him any more, she is in love with George Helmet, who has the longest legs in sixth grade. But Dad says today is a special treat because Aunt Deedee is here, even though I can tell Mom **DOES NOT** think it is a special treat, because normally Aunt Deedee is mostly saying things like, "Well if you buy cheap dish-washing detergent, then what do you expect?" Only today Aunt

Deedee says something completely brilliant and also **FORTUITOUS**, which is that strawberry smoothies are **NOT** a special treat when you are allergic to strawberries, which Georgia May Morton-Jones might be, and so she cannot have any she can only have water. And I say,

Aunt Deedee is right and maybe we should **ALL** have water in case we even breathe on Georgia May Morton-Jones and she **PERISHES** into her macaroni.

And Cosmo says, "Yes, good idea," even though strawberry smoothies are his second favorite drink after milk with mint syrup in it, which he says looks like alien ectoplasm but Daisy says looks like **GROSSNESS**. And so Mom takes away the strawberry smoothies even though I can tell she is not happy about it, and nor is Dad, who says he has been looking forward to it all day while Tony Juniper has been droning on about bus stops,

and nor is Daisy, who says it is against her **HUMAN RIGHTS** because she is very **BIG** on human rights as well as on being a celebrity chef.

And it turns out **NOR** is Mr. Bentley-Bucket because when Mom gives him his glass of water he does not drink any, not even a **DROP**. And so I say,

You should have a drink, Mr. Bentley-Bucket, or you will **PERISH** of thirst, unless you are a camel because they can go for weeks without water.

Only Mr. Bentley-Bucket says,

I'm fine, thank you, Penelope. I'm not a big water drinker.

And I **GASP**, and so does Cosmo, and he writes it down in his notebook because it is **STRANGE**.

And Mom says what is
with all the gasping and
writing? And I say it is
for school, which is not even
a lie. And Mom says well now is
NOT the time for writing but it **IS** time
for getting the Parmesan from the
kitchen, and can I please get it and
try to stay out of trouble.

And so I am getting the
Parmesan and not even going
near trouble, which I think is
probably the washing
machine, because it is still
broken from the time we
dyed Daisy's swan outfit blue,

when I have my next

BRILLIANT IDEA™,

which is to put garlic salt in the Parmesan cheese

because they are both yellow and powdery and

so it will be **INVISIBLE** and no one will be **ANY**

THE WISER, except Mr. Bentley-Bucket, and it

will not matter because he

will have **EVAPORATED**

INTO SMOKE.

And so I mix in the
garlic salt with the
cheese invisibly, and
I put in a lot so that
he will **EVAPORATE**
completely quickly,

and I take it in and say,

Would you like some Parmesan or are you not a big Parmesan eater?

And he says,

Actually, I am a fan of Parmesan.

And he puts a whole spoonful in his bowl.

And I **GASP** and so does Cosmo because I have whispered to him about the invisible garlic in the Parmesan, which Daisy says is rude, but Cosmo says is his **HUMAN RIGHT**. And Mom says,

Oh for heaven's sake, let's just eat.

And so everyone does except me and Cosmo, because we are waiting for the **EVAPORATION**.

And something **STRANGE** happens, only it is **NOT** evaporation, it is that Mr. Bentley-Bucket starts **COUGHING LIKE CRAZY**.

And so does Aunt Deedee.

And so does Barry, even though Mom told Gran macaroni and cheese is **NOT** for cats.

48

And Gran **GASPS** and says,

It is **POISONED CHEESE**,
I saw it on *Animal SOS!*

(Which is a program where
animals almost die but then they
don't and it is **MIRACULOUS**.)

But I say,

Do not fear, it is not poisonous for
MORTALS, only for **VAMPIRES**, because
I have secretly put invisible **GARLIC** in
the Parmesan and
any minute now
Mr. Bentley-Bucket
will **EVAPORATE**
before your **VERY
EYES**. Ta-dah.

And then everyone **GASPS**, only he does not evaporate, and I am racking my brain wondering why and so is Cosmo and he says maybe it is like Minimus Mayhem and he is super-powerful so it has to be garlic **AND** water, and I agree and so I throw a whole glass on his head, and so does Cosmo.

Only Mr. Bentley-Bucket **STILL** does not

evaporate, but there is a lot more **GASPING**,

and then a lot of shouting, and it is mostly at

me, because Aunt Deedee is upset that Mr.

Bentley-Bucket is wet and Mom is upset that

the floor is wet and Daisy is upset that the

macaroni and cheese is wet and also covered in

garlic. She says,

It is all your fault, Penelope Jones, you are such a complete **MORON**.

And Aunt Deedee says I am a
NINCOMPOOP and a **MENACE**
because Mr. Bentley-
Bucket is not a
VAMPIRE, he is a
BANK MANAGER.
And Mom says I am a
NINCOMPOOP and a
MENACE and **NUTS**
because vampires aren't
even real, they are completely
made-up, like aromatherapy and
miracle diets. And Dad
calls me Penny
Dreadful and does the
honking goose laugh.

But I do not see the funny side. And nor does Mom. And nor does Aunt Deedee.

★ ☆ ✸ ✦

But someone does, and that is Mr. Bentley-Bucket. Because the next day he sends me a letter saying that being mistaken for a vampire is the funniest thing that has ever happened to him, and here is a dollar coin and a book about foxes.

Dear Penny,
Being mistaken for a vampire is the funniest thing that has ever happened to me

FOXES

ALL ABOUT THEM

And I decide maybe being a clown isn't so bad after all.

But Cosmo is still being a vampire hunter because one of the bats on the church porch has pooped on his head, so it is definitely an **EVIL BEAST** and possibly a **VAMPIRE**.

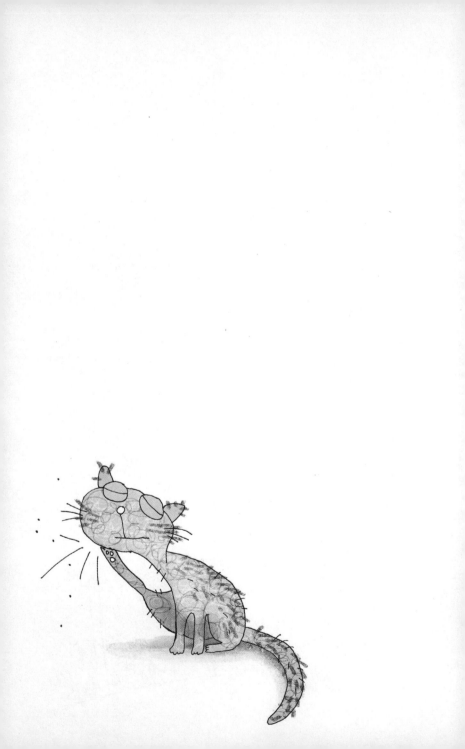

Sometimes I am completely **PLEASED AS PUNCH**, e.g. the time when me and Cosmo Moon Webster went to the wildlife park and we saw a monkey steal a sock and an ice cream.

Or the time me
and Dad had a
pancake-flipping
competition and his went
on top of the cabinet with the
broken toaster in it and mine went on the
ceiling, which meant I won even though it did
not come down for a whole hour until Mom
poked it with a broom.

But today I am not **PLEASED AS PUNCH**,
not even a **LITTLE** (even though it is winter
break, which is usually very **PLEASING**, because
Mr. Schumann cannot be **SICK AND TIRED** of
me). Instead I am completely **GLOOMY**.

What happens is when I get up I have a

BRILLIANT IDEA™,

which is that I will train Gran's cat Barry to be a
retriever cat, which means throwing things and
he will fetch them, e.g. a ball, or a newspaper, or
a rubber toy that looks like a duck.

Then he can be on *Pets Win Prizes*, which is a
television show where animals skateboard and
sometimes jump through hoops of fire (only Mom
says I am not allowed to do that, not **EVEN** over
her dead body), and he will win a gold medal

and a certificate and a year's supply of cat treats in the shape of fish. But I do not have a newspaper, because Dad is doing something important with it in the shed (and Mom says it had better not be reading it because he is supposed to be fixing the fence and he says it is absolutely not). And I do not have a ball, because it is somewhere in the next-door neighbor's yard and so is the rubber toy that looks like a duck. So I decide I will throw chocolate raisins because Barry likes chocolate raisins even though Mom says it is **CAT FOOD AND CAT FOOD ONLY**. And so I have thrown maybe a bazillion on the floor,

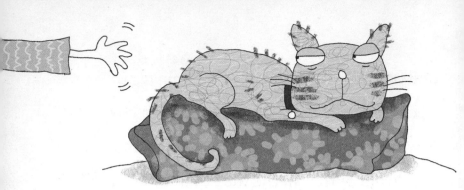

only Barry decides he does not want to fetch anything, not **EVEN** chocolate raisins. He wants to watch a show about cows on the television and so does my sister Daisy. And she says she can do what she likes because she is being the Queen of the Fairies in her school play next year and so it is important to practice being a queen **AT EVERY SECOND**, which means absolutely no helping me pick chocolate raisins off the carpet and absolutely lots of bossing. And so it is the **END OF THE WORLD**, which is why I am completely **GLOOMY**.

Gran says it is not the **END OF THE WORLD** and in fact I need to look on the **BRIGHT SIDE**, e.g. queens cannot eat chocolate raisins that have been on carpets. And so I am trying very hard to see the **BRIGHT SIDE** when the phone rings and I think ooh maybe it is Cosmo Moon Webster saying, "Do you want to invent a magic amulet that will transform Daisy into an amoeba that is smaller than a pea?" Only it is not, it is a lady who says it is Grandma from Baskerville and she is coming to stay for three days and she will be there by lunchtime. Goodbye.

And so I am completely **DISCOMBOBULATED** because my gran is not in Baskerville, she is on the sofa watching the show about cows, and so I go and see Dad, who is in the shed doing something with the newspaper which looks very much like reading. He says,

Why the long face, Jones?

I say it is because I am **GLOOMY** and also **DISCOMBOBULATED** and I tell him about the lady on the phone, and he turns very pale and almost immediately he calls Mom up at work, which is normally only allowed in an **EMERGENCY** because Dr. Cement does not like his phone lines clogged up (and no that does not mean when you want to know who is the tallest man in the whole world, for instance). But Dad says this is a definite **EMERGENCY** and amazingly Mom agrees because the grandma coming to stay is the **OTHER** grandma, i.e. Grandma Overall, who is Mom's mom and who is mostly upset with things and it is mostly with me because she does not see the **BRIGHT SIDE**, not once. And I am just thinking it is definitely the **END OF THE WORLD** and it cannot get **ANY WORSE**, when Mom gets home and says no Grandma Overall **CANNOT** share a room with Gran because they do not see **EYE TO EYE**, and in fact it is me and Daisy who will be doing the sharing and Grandma Overall can have Daisy's bed, and there is to be **NO** arguing and so it is completely **WORSE** and also the **END OF THE WORLD**.

Plus almost immediately we **ARE** arguing and not seeing **EYE TO EYE** and it is about who will sleep on the top bunk and I say it is me because I always sleep in the top bunk because I like to touch the ceiling with my nose and Daisy says it is her because she is the Queen and can do what she likes. Only Mom does not agree and says in fact no one can have the top bunk. She will put both mattresses on the floor and it will be great fun like camping, and we can do makeovers and whisper secrets to each other.

But Daisy says she would rather **PERISH** than tell me where her Rambling Rose lipstick is hidden. And I say I would rather **PERISH** than wear Rambling Rose lipstick and so in fact it is definitely the **END OF THE WORLD** and there is **NO BRIGHT SIDE** and for once Daisy agrees.

✷ ✩ ✷ ✹

And we are completely right because by lunchtime we are not seeing **EYE TO EYE** on what is better, a pink sparkle headband or a real actual plastic shark's tooth? And we are still arguing about the headband and the real actual plastic shark's tooth when the doorbell rings and it is not Cosmo Moon Webster again, it is Grandma Overall in a black hat, and so I am thinking that there is no **BRIGHT SIDE**, not anywhere.

And Grandma Overall thinks so too because
she says,

About time.
And what is that
strange man doing in
the front yard? He
looks like a **MORON**.

And I can tell Mom is also not looking on
the **BRIGHT SIDE** because her lips go very thin,
but she does not say so, she says,

That is Gordon.
He is fixing the
fence.

(Because it is broken from where me and Cosmo
tried to become mountaineers and scale Everest,
only Everest fell down onto some petunias.)
And Grandma says,

Well, he is making
a real pig's ear of
it. You should call
a professional.

And Mom
does not say
anything to
that, she puts
the kettle on.

Only Grandma says she does not drink tea after twelve because it gives her the **HEEBIE-JEEBIES**, and so Gran says, "How about a nice cup of coffee?" But Grandma says she does not drink coffee after ten in the morning because it still gives her the **HEEBIE-JEEBIES** and she would like a glass of water, but it has to be cold but not **COMPLETELY** cold, which luckily it is.

⭐ ⭐ ⭐ ⭐

And by bedtime no one is looking on the
BRIGHT SIDE, not **EVEN** Gran, who is normally
smiling even when it is raining **CATS AND DOGS**
because she says, "No point looking like a
WET WEEKEND, let's put our boots on and
pretend we are navigating the **SWAMP OF**

DOOM." But right now she is
looking definitely like a **WET**

WEEKEND and so is

Dad, and it is

because Grandma

Overall does not

want to sit on the

wobbly chair, she

wants to sit in the

green chair, which is normally where Dad sits and sleeps, only now he is on the wobbly chair and it has wobbled apart and so he has to make himself useful in the kitchen instead.

Mom says, "It will all be better in the morning, you will see." But I do not see because in the morning Grandma is still here and she is still not looking on the **BRIGHT SIDE** of anything, e.g.:

a) She does not like cats on the table, not **EVEN** if they are eating **CAT FOOD** and not Sugar Pops.

b) She does not
like Sugar Pops or
Choco Flakes or even Weety
Squares. She would like an apple,
but not if it has a wormhole or a
bruise, which it does, which is not
completely my fault. I was just trying
to see which bounced more, an apple or
a shoe, and it is the shoe.

3. She does not want to do any of my
BRILLIANT IDEAS™, not even the one where
we dress up as elks.

✷ ✩ ✦ ✦

And so I am completely seeing the **GLOOMY
SIDE** when the doorbell rings and I think it is
probably Mr. Schumann come to tell me he is

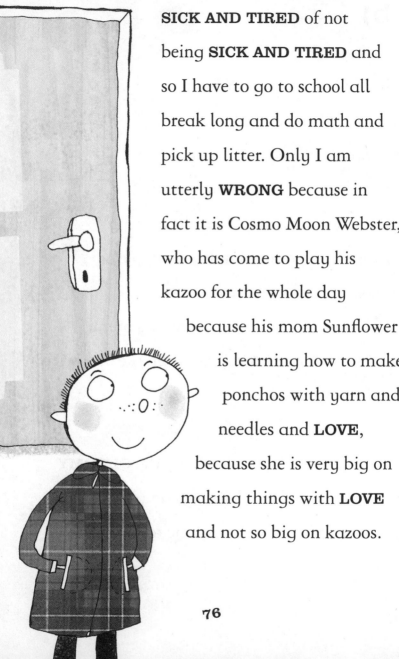

SICK AND TIRED of not being **SICK AND TIRED** and so I have to go to school all break long and do math and pick up litter. Only I am utterly **WRONG** because in fact it is Cosmo Moon Webster, who has come to play his kazoo for the whole day because his mom Sunflower is learning how to make ponchos with yarn and needles and **LOVE**, because she is very big on making things with **LOVE** and not so big on kazoos.

And nor is Grandma Overall, who says he had better not even **THINK** of tooting unless it is upstairs, because it will give her the **HEEBIE-JEEBIES** and also because it is time for her nap in the green chair.

And so we are in mine and Daisy's room, which is actually **MY** room (only Mom says not right now it is not) playing the kazoo and also Daisy's recorder with the bead stuck in the B hole, but it does not matter because the tune has a lot of Bs in it (and also because Daisy has gone to see Lucy B. Finnegan, who is her best friend, and who is only a **MINION** in the play, so she can boss her around instead).

Only Cosmo says it would be better if we could play the kazoo and recorder downstairs because then we could **CHARM** Barry with our music, because Cosmo is very **BIG** on charming animals with his music, especially snakes, only no one has one, and we are banned from the wildlife park for giving a sock and an ice cream to a monkey. And I say this is a

BRILLIANT IDEA™

because then Barry will definitely be on *Pets Win Prizes* and will get a gold medal and a certificate and a year's supply of cat treats

in the shape of fish. Only then I remember the
GLOOMY SIDE, which is Grandma Overall in
the green chair.

So Cosmo says it is not us who need to see the
BRIGHT SIDE, it is Grandma Overall, and it is
like Dr. Demonica (who is always freezing people
with her evil heart of ice, only Magnificent
Marvin melts her heart with his flame-throwing
fingers and she is nice to everyone until the next
episode when she swallows the reversal serum)
and all we have to do is **MELT** Grandma's heart.
And so then we are racking
our brains like **CRAZY**
thinking of things that
will melt Grandma's
heart and they are:

a) A cat that almost dies but doesn't, because on *Animal SOS*, cats are always cheering old ladies up by **MIRACULOUSLY** not dying, and then Griff Hunt, who is the presenter, shouts, "**THAT IS THE POWER OF PETS.**"

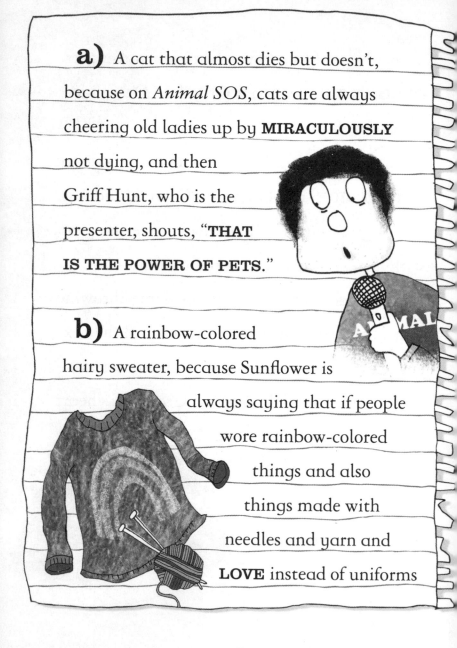

b) A rainbow-colored hairy sweater, because Sunflower is always saying that if people wore rainbow-colored things and also things made with needles and yarn and **LOVE** instead of uniforms and polyester then the world would be full of **JOY** instead of wars and melting ice caps.

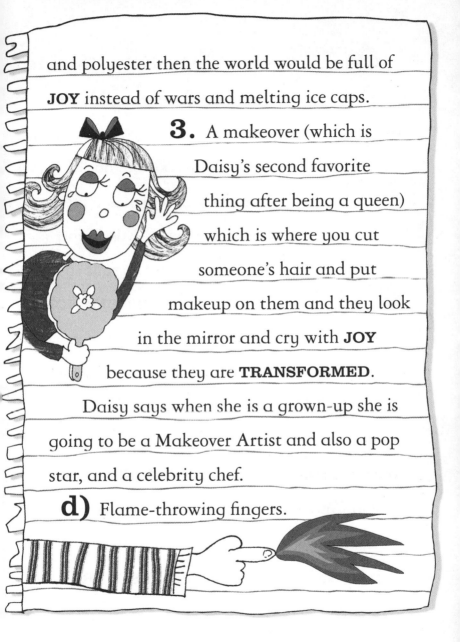

3. A makeover (which is Daisy's second favorite thing after being a queen) which is where you cut someone's hair and put makeup on them and they look in the mirror and cry with **JOY** because they are **TRANSFORMED**.

Daisy says when she is a grown-up she is going to be a Makeover Artist and also a pop star, and a celebrity chef.

d) Flame-throwing fingers.

Only our cat is Barry and Grandma Overall does not like Barry because he does not do cat things — he watches television and eats cereal — and also because his bottom has a piece of licorice stuck on it from where I was trying to give him two tails so he would be a **PHENOMENON**, but Grandma says it is not **PHENOMENAL**, it is unhygienic. And she also does not like rainbow-colored sweaters because she says people who wear them give her the **HEEBIE-JEEBIES**, e.g. Cosmo. And we do not have flame-throwing fingers and we have tried for almost five minutes, so it is definitely the **MAKEOVER**.

And we are looking everywhere for Daisy's Rambling Rose lipstick, only it is completely not to be seen, which I say is the **END OF THE WORLD** but which Cosmo says is just a **HURDLE TO BE OVERCOME**, because he is very into overcoming hurdles and also looking on the **BRIGHT SIDE**. And it turns out there **IS** a **BRIGHT SIDE**, which is that I have a pink marker, and also a blue one for eyeshadow and a black one for massive eyelashes, because Daisy says massive eyelashes are the most important part of the makeover, apart from the haircut. Only we decide we are not going to do a haircut because I am still in trouble from the time I accidentally let Georgia May Morton-Jones shave all her hair off, but we **WILL** make it look pretty with the sparkly headband. And so all we need to do now is tell Grandma Overall it is makeover time.

Only when we get downstairs Grandma Overall is still having her nap in the green chair,

which I say is the **END OF THE WORLD** but Cosmo says is just another **HURDLE** and we will **OVERCOME** it by doing her makeover while she is completely asleep and then she will wake up **TRANSFORMED** and her heart will melt **DOUBLY** quickly and she will be **DOUBLY** full of **JOY**.

And we are seeing completely **EYE TO EYE** and also scooting upstairs to get all the markers and the headband and also some yellow yarn (because in makeovers having yellowish hair, which is called blonde, is a very important part of being beautiful, and I think we can glue it onto the headband and make her possibly even **TRIPLY** full of joy), and then we scoot back down to start the makeovering.

And it is maybe the best makeover **EVER**, because I do nice big pink lips and round pink cheeks with the pink marker, and blue eyeshadow with the blue marker, and then Cosmo says it is his turn and I say it is not and he says it is because it is **OPPRESSIVE** against boys not to let him do makeovering and so he does the black eyelashes with the black felt-tip, and also a skull and crossbones on her forehead, which I say Grandma Overall will not like, but he says she will just think it is a mole because it is all wonky anyway. Then last of all we stick the yellow yarn to the headband and we put it on Grandma's head and then we get the mirror and we wait for her to wake up so we can shout **TA-DAH** and she will be full of **JOY** because she is blonde and beautiful.

We do not have to wait long
because something happens,
which is that Dad has
hammered a piece of himself
instead of the fence and so
he shouts.

And that makes
Barry, who is pooping
under the petunias,
run inside to jump

88

on Gran's lap, only it is the wrong gran, i.e. it is Grandma Overall. And she wakes up and sees herself in the mirror and screams which is maybe her heart melting or some **JOY**, which is when Mom and Daisy walk in because they are back from Lucy B. Finnegan's, because Lucy does not want to be bossed around, she wants to play badminton.

And I can tell Mom is not at all looking on the **BRIGHT SIDE** because she says,

And I say I have makeovered her and now she is beautiful and her heart has melted and she will not be upset with an apple with a bruise ever again. Only Grandma definitely does not look like her heart has melted, because she is rubbing at the skull and crossbones and it is completely not coming off and nor is the sparkle headband with the yellow yarn,

and Mom says,

Please tell me you did not use the markers that do not wash off.

So I say,

I did not use the markers that do not wash off.

And Mom says,

Is that true?

And I say,

No.

And then there is a lot more shouting and it is from Grandma Overall who says it is the **END OF THE WORLD**, and from Mom, who says it is **TYPICAL**, and from Daisy, who says it is all my fault because I am a complete **MORON**.

Only for once I see the **BRIGHT SIDE**, which is that Grandma Overall decides she has done enough visiting and goes back to Baskerville,

and so Daisy and me get our bedrooms back
and Dad gets the green chair back and Mom
gets some peace and quiet back, and so we are
all seeing **EYE TO EYE** and are completely
full of **JOY**.

Mr. Schumann is our principal, and he is mostly **SICK AND TIRED** all day, e.g.:

1. At **LUNCHTIME** when he says, "Penelope Jones, I am **SICK AND TIRED** of telling you to stop flicking peas onto the ceiling with a ruler."

99

Even though I was not flicking them at the ceiling I was flicking them at Bridget Grimes (who is the star student in our class and Mr. Schumann's favorite), only I am not very good at flicking peas, unlike Cosmo Moon Webster, who once got one to go right up Henry Potts's nose.

2. In PE when he says, "Penelope Jones, I am **SICK AND TIRED** of telling you that hoops are for twirling, not for hoopla-ing Alexander Pringle." Even though it is ten points for hoopla-ing Alexander Pringle and twenty points for hoopla-ing Mr. Eggs, who is our janitor and who smells like dogs, but no one has ever done that, not even Cosmo.

c) In **ASSEMBLY** when he says, "Penelope Jones, I am **SICK AND TIRED** of telling you that bottoms are for sitting on, not for shuffling." Even though assembly is just hymns, and Bridget Grimes playing "All Things Bright and Beautiful" on a recorder, and gold stars for excellence, which is almost never me, which is why it is so hard to keep my bottom still, which is why he is **SICK AND TIRED**. So if you think about it, it is not even my fault.

But today in assembly my bottom is not shuffling even one bit and so Mr. Schumann is not **SICK AND TIRED** one bit and it is all because of the VIP.

What happens is we get into assembly and we can tell it is not **NORMAL**, because at the front instead of just Mrs. Fazarkeley with a piano and Bridget Grimes with a recorder and Mr. Schumann with a hymn book and a tambourine and a mustache, there is another man who does not have a mustache or a hymn book or any instrument at all, but he does have a red hat and a **MYSTERIOUS** bag.

And almost immediately there is a lot of "ooh"ing and "aah"ing and Mr. Schumann has to do a lot of "shush"ing and then he says,

And it turns out that Bridget Grimes **DOES** know what that means and it is Very Important Person, **NOT** Very Interesting Pants, which is what Cosmo says. And so then we are all wondering like **CRAZY** who the VIP is, e.g.:

i) Henry Potts says he is a man who has been bitten by a shark and has lived to tell the tale, because Henry is very into sharks.

ii) Cosmo says he is a man who has been bitten by a herd of evil orcs and has lived to tell the tale, because Cosmo is very into evil orcs.

3. Bridget Grimes says he is Mort Hunter, who has won the world record for spinning plates, and it is 109.

And **AMAZINGLY** and also **ANNOYINGLY** Bridget Grimes is **RIGHT**, because the man has not been bitten by anything but he **IS** Mort Hunter. And so he opens his **MYSTERIOUS** bag and gets out some poles and some plates and does some spinning, only not with 109 plates but with six, because there is no room because of Mrs. Fazarkerley and her piano.

And there is even more "ooh"ing and "aah"ing, and also some "ouch"ing because one of the plastic plates flies off and hits Bridget Grimes on the nose (which I did not expect to happen, I was just seeing what would happen if I pinged the pole), which is when Mr. Schumann looks like he might be **SICK AND TIRED** after all and so might Mort Hunter, because he puts the plates and poles back in his **MYSTERIOUS** bag.

And then there is a lot of "*boo*"ing because the plates were the most **EXCITING** assembly **EVER**, only Mr. Schumann says that it is not the plates that are **EXCITING**. In fact the most **EXCITING** thing is that Mort Hunter used to go to St. Regina's school just like us. And so he is **LIVING PROOF** that we can all achieve something amazing if we put our minds to it (even Alexander Pringle, who is not putting his mind to anything but is putting his mouth to a jelly sandwich).

And then we are all "ooh"ing and "aah"ing again and Mr. Schumann says he hopes Mort Hunter can be an **INSPIRATION** to all of us, and then one day we can be in **ASSEMBLY** as **SHINING EXAMPLES**.

And Mr. Schumann is right, because as soon as I get back to class I am completely **INSPIRED** and wanting to be a **SHINING EXAMPLE** by breaking the world record for the longest time a spoon is balanced on my nose, because I can do eleven seconds before it falls in my soup, which Dad says is amazing and Mom says is another mess to clean up.

And everyone else is also wanting to be

SHINING EXAMPLES, e.g.:

1. Luke Bruce wants to grow the world's longest cucumber and it will be thirty-four inches long.

b) Henry Potts says he is going to grow the world's longest cucumber and it will be thirty-four *feet* long.

c) Cosmo says he is going to breed the world's biggest caterpillar and it will eat Henry's cucumber.

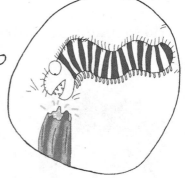

4. Henry says Cosmo has already broken a world record for the smallest brain and it is smaller even than a pea.

5. Bridget Grimes says she has already broken a world record and it is for the longest time playing a recorder and it is one hour and two minutes so she is **ALREADY** a **SHINING EXAMPLE**.

f) Brady O'Grady says he is going to break Bridget Grimes's world record by playing his recorder for a bazillion hours and two minutes and he will be the **SHINING EXAMPLE** and she will be only **SECOND**.

Which is when Bridget starts crying and when Miss Patterson says it would be a lot easier if we just did one world record between all of us, then we can **ALL** be a **SHINING EXAMPLE** and it can be the most children standing on one leg for at least a minute and we can do it tomorrow instead of our topic. And I am **PLEASED AS PUNCH** because I am excellent at standing on one leg.

And also because our topic is famous inventors and we are making a collage of Alexander Fleming, only I am not allowed to be in charge of the glue, because I had an argument with Bridget Grimes about whether penicillin has eyes and I glued her hair on a piece of Alexander Fleming's pants and Miss Patterson had to snip it out.

So the next morning we all troop to the cafeteria with Miss Patterson, and Mr. Schumann troops in as well because he is going to be **ADJUDICATOR**, which means he is in charge of who is standing on one leg and who is touching the floor with the tip of their shoe. And also there is going to be no leaning against walls, or leaning against other people, or dangling from the PE ropes. Or eating jelly sandwiches, which Alexander Pringle says is not fair because in fact he is trying to break the world record for standing on one leg while eating a jelly sandwich, so it will be **TWO** records in one if you think about it. And then Brady O'Grady says in that case he will also flip chips into his mouth while standing on one leg and then it will be **THREE** records. And Henry Potts says he will flip chips at Brady O'Grady so then it will be **FOUR** records.

Only Mr. Schumann says it is **ONE** record, and there will be absolutely no jelly or chips or flipping of any sort, and we are starting now.

"On your marks, get set, **GO**!"

And then I am utterly balancing on one foot and so is Cosmo, and so is Bridget Grimes and so is everyone else, except for Mr. Schumann, who is very busy **ADJUDICATING**, i.e. he is looking at his watch and also at Brady O'Grady, who is putting his toe completely close to the floor, which Bridget says is cheating and Brady O'Grady says is not and Bridget says is and Mr. Schumann measures and it is not.

And then we have been balancing **FOREVER**, i.e. almost **THIRTY** seconds, when a bad thing happens, which is that I need to use the restroom, so I put my hand up, which makes me go completely wobbly but I do **NOT** put my toe on the floor for even a second and Mr. Schumann says what is it and I say I need the restroom and he says I will have to wait. I say I can't but it is okay because I will hop all the way and it will not be cheating, but Bridget says it will be

and I say,

Won't.

And she says,

Will.

And Mr. Schumann says,

Oh just go and hurry up about it.

So I do.

1.

And I am hopping like **CRAZY**, i.e. I hop into the restroom...

2.

and then out of the restroom...

3.

and then to the sink...

120

4.

and then to
the door...

5.

and then back to
the sink because
I forgot to turn
the faucet off...

6.

and then I hop all
the way back to
the cafeteria again.

And I am thinking that I am completely **BRILLIANT** at standing on one leg and also hopping and maybe I will go everywhere like this **FOREVER** and I will win an Olympic race for hopping and be a **SHINING EXAMPLE**, when Bridget Grimes puts her hand up and says,

But Mr. Schumann, Penelope Jones is on the wrong leg.

And I am completely **DISCOMBOBULATED** and so is Mr. Schumann, who says there is not a wrong leg, only a right leg and a left leg and it does not matter which I am on. But Bridget says when I went to the restroom I was on the left leg and now I am on the right leg, which is the **WRONG** leg. And I look down and she is right, I am definitely on the right leg but I do not think it is the **WRONG** leg and I say so.

And so does Cosmo and so does Henry Potts, which is amazing because normally they do not agree on anything, not even that Maximus Terror, who is leader of the zombiebots, is taller than Minimus Mayhem, which he is. And that is when it all goes **WRONG** because Henry flicks something at Bridget Grimes, but it is not a chip, it is a chocolate-covered raisin that is in his pocket, and it hits her on the nose and she starts to wobble like **CRAZY** and is about to topple over

and everyone is "ooh"ing and "aah"ing, which
is when I decide I will be a **SHINING EXAMPLE**
by **SAVING BRIDGET** before she puts her foot
on the floor and so I run completely quickly and
push her back up again and she is still on one
leg and everyone cheers and I am **PLEASED
AS PUNCH**. But someone is not and that is Mr.

Schumann, who says
I am now definitely
on the **WRONG** leg,

which is not the right leg, it is the left leg this time, and so it is only one minute and forty-three seconds and that is not a record and so it is back to Alexander Fleming's pants for the rest of the morning.

And so everyone is completely **GLOOMY** but I am most **GLOOMY** of all, and I am **GLOOMY** all the way home and I am **GLOOMY** all through dinner, even though it is ham and beans, and I am **GLOOMY** in my dream, even though it is about a meerkat named Herman. And I am **DOUBLY GLOOMY** at breakfast on Saturday because it is toast with no butter because Barry has sat on it and it is all hairy.

Only that is when the doorbell rings and it is
Cosmo, who says he has come to cheer me up
with his

BRILLIANT IDEA™,

and we will definitely be

SHINING EXAMPLES and

be in the **ASSEMBLY**.

And he is right because his idea is very **BRILLIANT**, i.e. it is to completely make up a new record, because then we will be the first people in the book of records even if it is for only one minute forty-three seconds, and so my **GLOOM** is gone completely, because we are too busy racking our brains to think of new and **BRILLIANT** records and we think of three and they are:

1. Cut out the most pictures of cats in clothes from a newspaper **EVER**.

b) Fit the most cans of soup in the washing machine **EVER**.

3. Build the tallest tower out of some cans of soup, a jar of jam and a plastic horse with one eye **EVER**.

Only the scissors are in the **OUT OF BOUNDS** drawer for a lot of reasons, and the washing machine is not in the **OUT OF BOUNDS** drawer but it is definitely **OUT OF BOUNDS** for a lot of reasons, and so it is the tower or nothing. So we decide to do the tower in the kitchen on the table, because Daisy is busy in the living room sulking because she is not allowed to have a dress made of sparkle even though Lucy B. Finnegan has one. And Mom does not even say no we cannot because she is busy arguing with Dad over whether or not he is allowed to unclog the toilet, which has one of my socks in it, or whether they will call

Mr. Hose, even though Dad says he could
have been a plumber if he hadn't met Mom,
but she says he could not because he does not

know a monkey

wrench from

a monkey.

And when Gran comes into the kitchen, she does not say no we cannot because she is very **INTO** world records because her friend Arthur Peason once broke a record and it was for sucking up crispy puffs with a straw and putting them on a plate in a minute.

And the tower is going
~**FANTASTICALLY**~
because at the bottom there is a can of peas,

and then it is a can of beans, then cream of asparagus soup, then tomato soup and then a can of chicken, and a can of mandarin oranges, and then the jam, which is blueberry. And by then the tower is completely taller than my head and also very teetery but Cosmo says it is

not teetery it is **VICTORIOUS** and also a **SHINING EXAMPLE** and so it is time to put the horse with one eye on and measure it and then it will also be a **WORLD RECORD** and so on goes the horse and it is now actually very teetery and

so I get the tape measure completely quickly
and I measure by standing on a chair on my
tiptoes on one leg and it is the right leg. Only
then I am thinking that actually it might
be the **WRONG** leg because I **WOBBLE**,

and so the horse with one eye **WOBBLES**, and
then the jar of blueberry jam **WOBBLES**, and
then the can of mandarin oranges **WOBBLES**,
and then all the soup **WOBBLES**, and
then there is a big enormous noise and
it **ALL FALLS DOWN**. Which is when
Mom and Dad and Daisy and
Gran all come in to see what
the hoo-hah is.

And it is very definitely
a hoo-hah because
there is jam on the
ironing board,

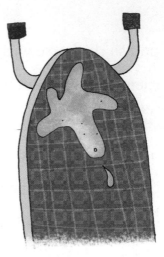

and the horse with one
eye is upside down in
Barry's cat food,

and the can of mandarin
oranges has hit the tricky
faucet and the tricky
faucet handle has poinged
off and there is water
spraying on the ceiling,

which means
Mom does have
to call Mr. Hose
after all.

Daisy says,

It is all your fault,
Penelope Jones. You are
such a complete **MORON**.

But for once I do not care, because the tower was thirty-four inches tall, which means it will be in the record books, and so I am a **SHINING EXAMPLE** and so is Cosmo Moon Webster.

The End

Or at least until next Tuesday, which is when a man in China named Ho Lee makes a soup and jam and horse tower and it is thirty-eight inches because he had a can of potato too.

Everybody Loves Penny!

"Penny is an exciting and entertaining character who always has **BRILLIANT IDEAS**... If Penny was my **BFF** then life would never be dull."

Rachel, age 9

"Penny Dreadful stories are very funny and exciting. It is a fantastic series."

Polly, age 10

"I liked Penny because she's naughty, but in a way she's also funny too! I did not like Mrs. Butterworth because she's got a mustache."

Millie, age 8

"I think Penny Dreadful is, well, dreadfully funny. (She sounds like my brother — hee hee.) PS I'm turning a little dreadful too."

Islay, age 8

"I think Penny Dreadful is a great book! I learned 'e.g.' means 'for example'. I learned 'i.e.' means 'that is'."

Bryn, age 8

"A hilariously funny read!"

Anastasia, age 11

"I loved Penny Dreadful, especially in **'PENNY DREADFUL BECOMES A HAIRSTYLIST'**. And the lady with the mustache. Fantastico!"

Leila, age 7

"I love Penny Dreadful, she is brilliant and very funny."

Iona, age 6

"I wanted to read on and on and on...it was _soooo_ good."

Matt, age 8

"This book is funny and full of **BRILLIANT IDEAS** and I like the way it uses **'E.G.'** all the time!"

Megan Emily, age 6

"Here are some of the things I enjoyed about the book:

1. I liked it when Penny and Cosmo tried to shave Barry the cat (the coolest cat ever).
b) Does Penny ever comb her hair?
3. Where did Cosmo get his Jedi suit... I want one!
iv. I liked Mrs. Butterworth at the general store and her mustache!"

Gruffudd, age 10

Joanna Nadin

wrote this book —
and lots of others
like it. She is small,
funny, clever,
sneaky and musical.
Before she became a writer, she wanted to be a
champion ballroom dancer or a jockey, but she
was actually a lifeguard at a swimming pool,
a radio newsreader, a cleaner in an old people's
home, and a juggler. She likes peanut butter on
toast for breakfast, and jam on toast for dessert.
Her perfect day would involve baking, surfing,
sitting in cafes in Paris, and playing with
her daughter — who reminds her a lot
of Penny Dreadful…

Jess Mikhail

illustrated this book. She loves creating funny characters with bright colors and fancy patterns to make people smile.

Her favorite place is her tiny home, where she lives with her tiny dog and spends lots of time drawing, scanning, scribbling, printing, stamping, and sometimes using her scary computer. She loves to rummage through a good charity shop to find weird and wonderful things. A perfect day for her would have to involve a sunny beach and large amounts of spicy foods and ice cream (not together).

For Juno Nadin,
who I am quite sure will
be a record breaker.

First published in the UK in 2013 by Usborne Publishing Ltd., Usborne House,
83-85 Saffron Hill, London EC1N 8RT, England. www.usborne.com

Copyright © Joanna Nadin, 2013
Illustrations copyright © Usborne Publishing Ltd., 2013

A CIP catalogue record for this book is available from the British Library.

First published in America in 2015 AE.

PB ISBN 9780794529925
ALB ISBN 9781601303523
FMAMJJASOND/15 02843/6
Printed in Dongguan, Guangdong, China.

Penny Dreadful

is a Record Breaker

By Joanna Nadin   Illustrated by Jess Mikhail

Contents